CHINESE MYTHS

AN ILLUSTRATED COLLECTION

The Beginning
Volume 1 • Stories 1-5 of 25

Retold by Toby Johnson
Illustrated by Hao
Edited by Marie Furnary

ENJOY THE ENTIRE COLLECTION

VOLUME 2 | DISCOVERY

Stories include:
- Loyal Fuxi
- Shennong Feeds and Heals
- Huangdi's Cart
- Leizu Spins Silk
- Scholar Ling Makes Music

VOLUME 4 | YAO SHUN YU

Stories include:
- Houyi Shoots the Sun Crows
- Good Mother Xiwangmu
- Chang'e Shoots to the Moon
- Shun's Missions
- Yu Thrusts Back the Floods

VOLUME 3 | CIVILIZATION

Stories include:
- Chiyou Raids Huangdi
- Scholar Cang Creates Writing
- Bird Nation
- Chenxiang's Vow
- A Princess' Tale

VOLUME 5 | SEA DRAGONS

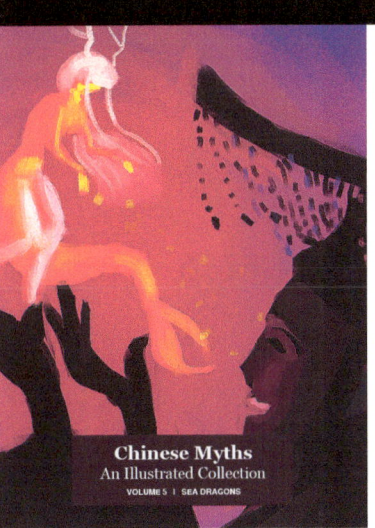

Stories include:
- The Sea King Invades
- Nezha Bothers the Sea King
- Eight Gods' Paths Across the Sea
- Gold, Gems, and Dragons
- The Prince and Beijing's Water

USA English Limited (Hong Kong)

Floor 20, Mongkok Commercial Centre,
16 Argyle Street,
Mongkok, Hong Kong
Tel: +852 35881716
E-mail: info@usaenglish.org
Website: www.usaenglish.org

Chinese Myths: An Illustrated Collection
Volume 1 | The Beginning
© USA English Limited (Hong Kong)

Retold by Toby Johnson
Illustrated by Hao
Edited by Marie Furnary

Research Consultant: Junzhe Gao
Design: Alexandra Sieh

ISBN: 978-1-953939-00-5

TABLE OF CONTENTS

PANGU FORMS THE LAND AND SKY

《盘古开天辟地》

PRONUNCIATION GUIDE

(FOR CHINESE NAMES IN THIS STORY)

CHINESE NAME	PRONUNCIATION
Pangu (盘古)	pan-goo

According to lore, at the start of it all, before fish swam in blue seas and birds soared across bright skies; before any people were even born ...

All was black. All was dark.

There was nothing but an egg.

In the center of this enormous egg sat a gigantic god named Pangu.

Without an exit or a floor, Pangu could not decide which way was up or down. Pangu was bored. He wanted out.

Pangu used a sharp ax to rip and tear the walls of his prison. With gigantic force, Pangu's ax tore the egg apart. It leaked clear stuff and dark stuff.

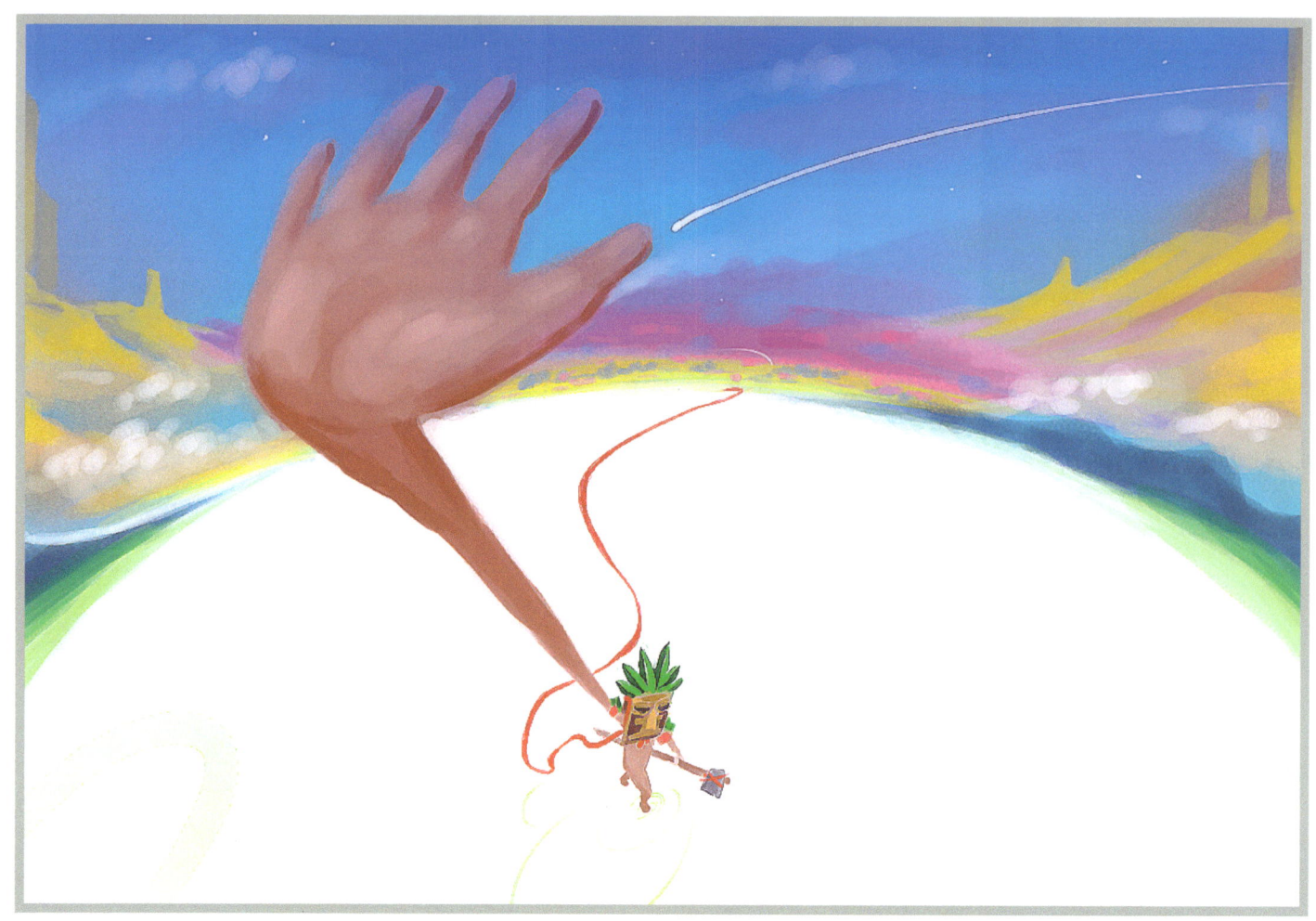

For many years, Pangu pushed the two types of egg-goo apart.

With his legs, Pangu forced the dark substance down to form rich earth. With his arms, Pangu pressed the clear stuff up, creating transparent sky.

As he pushed down the earth, Pangu grew taller and
taller, stretching the sky upward. After many years,
he rested, no longer forcing earth and sky apart.

Now Pangu was sole lord of a large, lonely world.
His body ached, and he longed for someone to talk to.

Without friends or family, Pangu let out one last breath, and died. There was no one to mourn him. Pangu's corpse transformed parts of his barren world. His right eye drifted far up into the clear sky as a sun, lighting dark earth below like a brilliant torch. His left eye remained in the transparent sky, too, shining through each night as a soft moon. His whiskers became sparkling stars. Pangu's hair cascaded down, forming lush trees, grasses, and various plants on the wide earth. His arms and legs created rolling hills and steep mountains.

Pangu's blood flowed over the land as rippling rivers, as tranquil lakes, as sorrowful seas. His flesh became dark, rich loam for farming rice, corn, gourds, and all delicious crops. His teeth and bones, absorbed by the earth, formed gold and silver, as well as other precious metals. His bones transformed into hard rocks and gorgeous gemstones.

Pangu's last breath floated over his fresh world, as winds, clouds, and storms that blow through our lands even today.

NÜWA PREPARES PEOPLE

《女娲造人》

PRONUNCIATION GUIDE

(FOR CHINESE NAMES IN THIS STORY)

CHINESE NAME	PRONUNCIATION
Nüwa (女娲)	new-wah
Pangu (盘古)	pan-goo

The world Pangu created was a great, wild place. Both moon and sun inhabited the sky, while stars sparkled all around.

Mountains, rivers, grasslands, and forests covered the land. Before long, animals appeared in the infant world. Bugs, fish, birds, and beasts roamed the wide earth. Bears played in verdant forests; hares hopped through swaying grasslands. Snakes hid in dark lairs; bugs buzzed in fragrant air near pear trees.

Then, the goddess Nüwa arrived in the fair world.

She appeared as a beautiful woman with long black hair. Her black eyes flared with life spark. Although she seemed like a person, a snake's tail whipped from her waist, replacing long legs with slinky scales.

As a friend to the infant world, she treated all plants and animals with absolute care. The bears, the hares, even the pear trees were gently left in peace. Nüwa just stared at her amazing world.

Although the world was full of great wonders, Nüwa felt alone. She saw no one like her.

Nüwa found a translucent lake, and gazed at her reflection in the clear water.

Nüwa had a beautiful face, and soft, full hair, but she felt unusual and rare.

Nüwa prepared clay from the moist lake soil and formed people who looked like her. She kindly gave each person a pair of legs instead of a scaly tail, so they could walk across the dry earth.

Nüwa formed men and women, then breathed life-giving air into her humans, and watched them awaken into life.

One day, some of the first people Nüwa had made were still. They had died. She needed to make more people.

Nüwa became scared that she would never be able to stop forming people.

So, she allowed the women and men to make their own families with children. As the children grew, they formed families of their own.

People filled the earth, and inhabited all the lands.

At last, Nüwa could rest.

She watched her little friends live out wondrous lives, spreading humanity across Pangu's peaceful earth.

GONGGONG STRIKES BUZHOU MOUNTAIN

《共工怒触不周山》

PRONUNCIATION GUIDE
(FOR CHINESE NAMES IN THIS STORY)

CHINESE NAME	PRONUNCIATION
Buzhou (不周)	boo-jo
Gonggong (共工)	gong-gong
Nüwa (女娲)	new-wah
Zhurong (祝融)	jew-rong

After Nüwa created humans, Zhurong, the peaceful God of Fire, arrived on earth with his son, the terrifying God of Water, Gonggong. The God of Fire loved peace; but Zhurong and his son were not alike.

When young Gonggong wanted to fight, he rode his dragon across the sky, frightening all the other gods. It delighted Gonggong to terrify the gods.

Of all the great gods and goddesses, only his own father could stop him with a secret skill. From his own dragon, Zhurong could shoot bright fire from his mouth at the speed of light.

Gonggong craved his father's mighty skill, but Zhurong refused to share this powerful mystery with his war-hungry son.

Each night, Gonggong trained in fighting with a pair of sharp axes. He thought that, if only he could strike his father out of the heavens, he could use the force of all the world's water to pry the secret of this fire skill from Zhurong.

After many nights of training, Gonggong climbed onto his fierce dragon, flying right at Zhurong with his mighty axes. With a big swing, one ax struck Zhurong's thigh. The Fire God sighed, falling toward the earth in his son's tight grip. Father and son fell with their dragons into earth's dense clouds. Hidden in the white mist, Gonggong stood upright on the back of his dragon first. From that vantage point, he swung another ax, aiming to smite his own father's head. But Zhurong's fiery sword sliced up to stop that strike.

The two gods fought inside thick clouds for three days and three nights, lighting up the earth below with their fiery blows. Gonggong did not share Zhurong's stamina or skill. Hidden by thick clouds, he could not frighten his father into breathing the secret, bright fire.

So Gonggong lied. He asked for a truce, requesting that they meet at the bottom of Buzhou Mountain to talk. His lie of ending the vicious fight with words tricked his father, who wanted peace.

Although Zhurong was frightened for his son to be near people on Earth, his own desire for a peaceful end to the battle made him agree to talk. Both gods flew on their dragons down to the trembling earth. There, the son turned his lips into a tight, sly smile.

As the Water God, he used his own secret power to pull all the world's water from seas, lakes, and rivers. He sucked the Yellow River and the Long River dry, forcing the earth's combined water to fly in a powerful stream toward Zhurong.

His father's eyes filled with fright. Gonggong smiled slyly. His father's mouth opened wide. All the world's mighty water spouted toward Zhurong. There was only one thing the father could do to stop its destruction.

"Show me your secret skill, Father!" cried Gonggong. But, as Zhurong's bright fire began to burn away the forceful water, Gonggong could not see, because of the fire's blinding light. "Nooooo!" Gonggong cried. His burning eyes closed in pain as he fled back toward the dark sky.

Thrashing, blind Gonggong crashed into Buzhou Mountain, which tipped slightly, its peak slicing open the sky. Fire and water poured through, tormenting the earth below, and ravaging the lands for days.

Full of love and pity for her people, the goddess Nüwa returned from her place of rest to heal the world once again.

NÜWA PATCHES THE SKY WITH SWIRLS

《女娲补天》

PRONUNCIATION GUIDE

(FOR CHINESE NAMES IN THIS STORY)

CHINESE NAME	PRONUNCIATION
Buzhou (不周)	boo-jo
Gonggong (共工)	gong-gong
Nüwa (女娲)	new-wah
Zhurong (祝融)	jew-rong

Buzhou Mountain was one of four sturdy towers that held up the sky.

After Water God Gonggong fought with his father, Zhurong, Buzhou Mountain tipped a little to one side, ripping the sky wide open.

Torrents of water, nasty germs, and molten fire surged out of this new hole in the sky.

The forceful water caused rivers to churn, flooding the helpless land. Dirty germs made people sick. Hot, whirring winds set fires, which burned whole forests.

Scaly serpents and ferocious tigers crept from burning forests, terrifying the goddess Nüwa's people.

The gods' battle of fire and water cursed the entire world.

The goddess Nüwa had created the first humans herself from soft river clay, so she yearned to help her powerless people.

First, Nüwa made a stove from dirt, creating a hot fire inside. She put a large urn over this blazing furnace.

Next, Nüwa placed pretty rocks and colorful minerals into her pot. Stirring the rocks and minerals together over bright heat, Nüwa swirled their colors into shades of sparkling pinks and purples in the great urn.

Nüwa patched the hole in the sky with her melted rocks and metals. After that, she raised Buzhou Mountain, setting the sky level once again. She also made firm the other three towers that helped hold up the sky. Under each sky tower, Nüwa placed a monster turtle shell from the ocean floor, to make its base sturdy.

Nüwa fixed the beautiful pink and purple sky patch forever, so the land was no longer cursed with plagues.

Rivers no longer churned; forests ceased burning. Nasty germs, slinky serpents, and stealthy tigers stopped terrorizing human homes.

Girls and boys turned bright eyes up, admiring pretty pink and purple swirls in the evening sky.

They laughed in delight, saying, "Thank you, Nüwa!"

KUAFU CHASES THE SUN

《夸父追日》

PRONUNCIATION GUIDE

(FOR CHINESE NAMES IN THIS STORY)

CHINESE NAME	PRONUNCIATION
Kuafu (夸父)	kwah-foo
Nüwa (女娲)	new-wah
Pangu (盘古)	pan-goo
Wei (渭)	way
Yugu (禺谷)	yoo-goo

Long ago the world was wild, and Nüwa's poor people struggled to survive. There were no tools, so clever humans chipped stones into sharp cutting edges. With their stone blades, people whittled wood into hatchets, clubs, and hammers. They built huts.

Hungry children chased wild chickens, while their elders hunted small wild animals. In the deep forests, rabbits, foxes, and ravens fought for their lives against the new hunters.

On a huge mountain in the wild world, a clan of giant people lived. Their clan chief, the giant Kuafu, was the tallest, strongest chief in all China.

When they chose Kuafu for chief, his people gave him a strong wooden staff. Each day, Kuafu led the Kuafu Clan as they made tools, hunted animals, and fought wild beasts.

One year, the sun became very childish. As a golden crow, the sun flew close to the land, scorching it under devastating heat. The rivers, evaporating under this hot sun, gave up their waters.

The golden crow charred Kuafu's tall mountain black. People could not live on their parched earth. Kuafu promised to catch the naughty sun, and make him stop scorching all of Pangu's beautiful lands.

That night, Kuafu traveled to the far Eastern Sea with his staff. As the dawn cast a soft green glow in the east, Kuafu began to chase the childish sun crow across the morning sky.

Kuafu's giant legs carried him like a strong wind. "I can catch the sun, I can catch the sun," Kuafu whispered to himself. The clan chief chased the golden crow across China all day.

Kuafu did not stop for lunch. Picking cherries or peaches from wild orchards, he ate on the run. When he was thirsty, Kuafu sipped water from a river and kept up the chase. Becoming sleepy, he took short naps and kept chasing the sun. "I can catch the sun, I can catch the sun," Kuafu repeated silently.

Kuafu's legs stretched across tall mountains; Kuafu's legs bounded over wide rivers; Kuafu's legs breached deep canyons. "I can catch the sun, I can catch the sun," Kuafu sang, chasing the glowing golden crow.

Kuafu chased the sun to a place called Yugu. Moving in closer and closer, Kuafu at last reached out his hand to grab the golden crow. But just as his hand stretched out to touch the sun, he felt dizzy, and fainted from the heat. When Kuafu woke up, the sun was far to the west.

Even so, Kuafu did not give up. "I can catch the sun, I can catch the sun," Kuafu repeated, and started to run again. But Kuafu was parched from running so close to the sun. His lips were chapped and his chest was drenched with sweat.

Running past the Yellow River, Kuafu chugged all its water, but that did not quench his thirst.

Kuafu sucked up all the water in the Wei River, but his parched throat craved more. His chapped lips and parched throat ached for moisture. Kuafu lurched forward and died. Kuafu's body transformed into Kuafu Mountain.

His staff became a peach orchard, whose juicy fruit could quench any thirst. Although Kuafu did not catch the sun, the gods noticed his heroic sacrifice. The Jade Emperor, the most powerful god in all heaven, punished the sun crow, forcing him to stop scorching the earth. Celebrating their champion, Kuafu's clan moved their home to Kuafu Mountain. There, the clan had many children and lived happily. They ate peaches from fruitful orchards, and paid tribute to the Jade Emperor, who had recognized the honorable sacrifice of their cherished chief, Kuafu.

Chinese Myths: An Illustrated Collection
Volume 1: The Beginning
© USA English Limited (Hong Kong)
All Rights Reserved. www.phunics.com
Retold by Toby Johnson
Illustrated by Hao
Edited by Marie Furnary
Mongkok, Hong Kong
www.usaenglish.org

www.ingramcontent.com/pod-product-compliance
Lightning Source LLC
Chambersburg PA
CBHW040959170626
46815CB00002B/69